D0587299

FOR **TRISTAN,** ⭐
**JACK & POLLY,**
**FINLEY & ERIN**
...and **RAY** too!
A.S.

⭐

FOR
**MR S. WARREN** ⭐
who's seen them all.
J.W.

**TALENT SHOW THIS WAY** ➡
⭐

# Sing a Song of

PUFFIN BOOKS
Published by the Penguin Group: London, New York,
Australia, Canada, India, Ireland, New Zealand and South Africa
Penguin Books Ltd, Registered Offices: 80 Strand, London WC2R 0RL, England
puffinbooks.com    First published 2010
Text copyright © Jeanne Willis, 2010    Illustrations copyright © Adam Stower, 2010
Made and printed in China    ISBN: 978–0–141–32880–5    004

Sing a song of bottoms, cos everybody's got 'em
They come in every shape and every size.

Dogs have a waggy one.

Bears have a baggy one.

Monkeys have a brilliant backside.

Mice have teeny ones, titchy-witchy weeny ones.

And whales are very, very, very wide.

Rabbits have a puffy one. Squirrels have a fluffy one. Camels have a

humpy one, they say.

Kangaroos have jumpy ones.

Elephants have trumpy ones.

And peacocks love to put theirs on display.

Let's hear you...

Everyone's behind is perfectly designed
But which of them deserves to win the prize?

Let's
see
now...

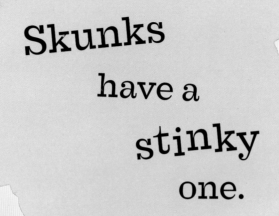

Skunks have a stinky one.

Squid have an inky one.

Rhinos have a **wrinkly** one, it seems.

Tortoises have crinkly ones.

Pigs have perky

pinky ones.

But pythons
only have them
in their dreams.

Clowns have
a silly one.

A princess has

a frilly one.

A snowman

has a **chilly** one,
poor chap.

Pirates have a jolly one.

Trolls? A fol-de-rol-y one –
every one of them deserves a clap.

That's
why
we . . .

Sing a song of bottoms, cos everybody's got 'em
They come in every shape and every size.

Everyone's behind is perfectly designed
But which of them deserves to win the prize?

I'll
tell
you...

Bats are the squeakiest.

Martians are the freakiest.

Babies are the cheekiest, it's true.

The judge
said after
**dinner,**

"Someone's sitting on a winner..."

# First prize goes to YOU!

**1**st

*This is to certify that*

# THE BEST BOTTOM

*belongs to:*